Postman Pat® and the
Great Greendale Race

SIMON AND SCHUSTER

It was early morning in Greendale, and Pat was collecting the letters from a postbox. "What a lovely peaceful day it is, Jess . . ."

Just then . . . VROOM! VROOM!
Ajay raced past on his motorbike.
"Goodness me, Jess! Look at Ajay go!"

At Thompson's Ground, Pat gave Alf his seed catalogue. "I was just saying to Jess, what a lovely peaceful . . ."

BEEP! BEEP!

Ted Glen zoomed past.

"By gum! Ted tears around in that lorry of his," said Alf. "But give me my reliable old tractor any day."

"And I'd never swap my trusty old van!" agreed Pat. "I know, Alf, why don't we have a Great Greendale Race around the village?"

"Count me in, Pat!"

Pat told everyone on his round about the Great Greendale Race.

"Julian says Ajay is sure to win!" Pat told Julia Pottage.

"Drivers have to use their heads as well as their accelerators, Pat!" said Julia. "Why not have some tests along the way – to find out who knows the Rules of the Road? I can get the children to help."

"What a grand idea!" said Pat.

It was the day of the Great Greendale Race.

Jeff Pringle gave the signal. "Ready . . . steady . . . go! And they're off!. . . Oh dear, where's PC Selby?"

PC Selby had a flat tyre! "Oh Da-ad! Hurry!" pleaded Lucy, as he pumped it up.

Ajay shot ahead.
Alf was in second place, crawling slowly up the narrow road on his tractor.

"Speed up, Alf!" groaned Ted. "We'll never catch up with Ajay!"

Ajay arrived at the first test stop.

"Right, Ajay," said Dorothy. "For this test, the children have made some road signs."

"And you have to tell us what they mean," added Bill.

"Well now," Ajay said, "that one looks like 'tunnel ahead' and I think the other one means 'slippery road'."

"Two out of two!" grinned Bill.

"I'd better get going then!" Ajay sped away.

Meanwhile, Pat and Alf had got into a pickle.

"Oo 'eck, which road, Pat?"

"This way, Alf!" called Pat, turning left.

Alf wasn't so sure. He turned right instead!

Ted pulled up in his lorry for the second test.

"Now, Mr Glen," said Katy and Tom Pottage, "we are traffic lights. When we hold up a coloured ball, you have to say what that colour means."

"Well, let me see . . . red means STOP! And green means GO! And orange means STOP! too, but that the lights will change any second."

"Yes!"

"These balls are great for juggling!" laughed Ted, throwing them up in the air. "Whoops! I've lost a traffic light in the bramble bush! I'll get it back in a jiffy."

PC Selby had just turned up on his bicycle. "Always approach bramble bushes with caution!" he said, looking at Ted's prickly hands.

"Ah well!' said Ted, cheerfully. "I'll carry on the race just as soon as I've got these prickles out."

"Your turn to take the test now, PC Selby," said the twins.

Alf soon realised he'd taken the wrong turning when he ended up at a rubbish dump! He turned his tractor around. "I'd better get a move on!" But just round the corner a flock of sheep had strayed onto the road. "Oh dear! Best get you safely back into your field!"

"Hello, Alf," said Pat. "Looks like we both took the wrong road. What's going on here then?"

"Just putting these sheep back where they belong, Pat. Don't mind me, try and catch up with Ajay."

"Righto, Alf. See you later!"

Pat arrived at the final test.

"This is to check your eyesight," said Dr Gilbertson. "Sarah has painted a picture. Can you see what it is?"

Pat peered across. "Mmm, it looks a bit like a teddybear . . . No. . . a dog!"

"Miaow!!" said Jess loudly.

"Oh, yes, silly me – it's Jess! Lovely picture, Sarah!"

Pat jumped back into his van. At the edge of the village, he saw Ajay pushing his motorbike along the road.

"I've run out of petrol!" sighed Ajay. "Don't stop, Pat, the winning line is just round the corner."

"Hang on a tick," said Pat, "I reckon I've got a can of petrol in the back of my van!"

Jess shook his head in despair!

PC Selby cycled up as Pat was checking in his van.

"Afternoon all! What's the problem?" he asked.

"I'm out of petrol," Ajay explained.

"Don't worry about us, Arthur," said Pat. "You carry on."

"Well, as long as all's well, I'll be on my way."

Jeff Pringle held up the chequered flag at the finishing line. "And, the winner of the Great Greendale Race is . . .

. . . PC Selby!

Alf is second. . . Ted third, Ajay's in fourth place . . . and last . . . is Pat!"

"You did it Dad!" cheered Lucy.

The Reverend Timms presented PC Selby with a trophy.

"Congratulations! Pedal-power has won the day!" he chuckled. "And now, a special prize. For helping Ajay, and losing his chance to win the race – I'd like to present Pat with one of Mrs Pottage's apple pies!"

"Thankyou!" Pat beamed. "Anyone for a slice?"

"Yes please!" said Julian. "And Dad . . . make sure you come last again next year!"

SIMON AND SCHUSTER
First published in 2005 in Great Britain by Simon & Schuster UK Ltd
Africa House, 64-78 Kingsway
London WC2B 6AH

Postman Pat® © 2005 Woodland Animations, a division of Entertainment Rights PLC
Licensed by Entertainment Rights PLC
Original writer John Cunliffe
From the original television design by Ivor Wood
Royal Mail and Post Office imagery is used by kind permission of Royal Mail Group plc
All rights reserved

Text by Alison Ritchie © 2005 Simon & Schuster UK Ltd

All rights reserved including the right of reproduction in whole or in part in any form

A CIP catalogue record for this book is available from the British Library upon request

ISBN 0 689 87557 6

Printed in China

3 5 7 9 10 8 6 4